DK READERS

D0359399

STAR WARS

Blast Off!

Get ready to meet
some exciting people
and creatures.

A Note to Parents

DK READERS is a compelling program for beginning readers, designed in conjunction with leading literacy experts, including Dr. Linda Gambrell, Professor of Education at Clemson University. Dr. Gambrell has served as President of the National Reading Conference and the College Reading Association, and has recently been elected to serve as President of the International Reading Association.

Beautiful illustrations and superb full-color photographs combine with engaging, easy-to-read stories to offer a fresh approach to each subject in the series. Each DK READER is guaranteed to capture a child's interest while developing his or her reading skills, general knowledge, and love of reading.

The five levels of DK READERS are aimed at different reading abilities, enabling you to choose the books that are exactly right for your child:

Pre-level 1: Learning to read
Level 1: Beginning to read
Level 2: Beginning to read alone
Level 3: Reading alone
Level 4: Proficient readers

The "normal" age at which a child begins to read can be anywhere from three to eight years old. Adult participation through the lower levels is very helpful for providing encouragement, discussing storylines, and sounding out unfamiliar words.

No matter which level you select, you can be sure that you are helping your child learn to read, then read to learn!

LONDON, NEW YORK, MUNICH,
MELBOURNE, AND DELHI

For Dorling Kindersley
Senior Editor Elizabeth Dowsett
Managing Art Editor Ron Stobbart
Managing Editor Catherine Saunders
Brand Manager Lisa Lanzarini
Publishing Manager Simon Beecroft
Category Publisher Alex Allan
Production Editor Siu Yin Chan
Production Controller Rita Sinha
Reading Consultant Dr. Linda Gambrell

For Lucasfilm
Executive Editor J. W. Rinzler
Art Director Troy Alders
Keeper of the Holocron Leland Chee
Director of Publishing Carol Roeder

Designed and edited by Tall Tree Ltd
Designer Jonathan Vipond
Editor Rob Colson

First published in the United States in 2010
by DK Publishing
375 Hudson Street, New York, New York 10014

12 13 14 10 9 8 7 6 5 4 3

DK books are available at special discounts when purchased in bulk
for sales promotions, premiums, fund-raising, or educational use.
For details, contact:
DK Publishing Special Markets
375 Hudson Street, New York, New York 10014
SpecialSales@dk.com

A catalog record for this book is available
from the Library of Congress.

ISBN: 978-0-7566-6692-7 (Paperback)
ISBN: 978-0-7566-6879-2 (Hardback)

Reproduced by Media Development and Printing Ltd., UK
Printed and bound in China by L.Rex Printing Company Limited

Discover more at:
www.dk.com
www.starwars.com

Contents

5... 4... 3... 2... 1...
Blast off!

Meet Anakin Skywalker.
He is a Jedi Knight.

lightsaber

Anakin

Meet R2-D2.
He is a droid.
He can fix other droids.

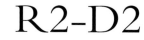

R2-D2

Meet C-3PO.

He is a droid.

He can speak many
languages.

C-3PO

Padmé

Meet Padmé Amidala.
She is a Senator.

Obi-Wan

Meet Obi-Wan
Kenobi. He is a
Jedi Master.

beard

Meet Yoda. He is the
most powerful Jedi.

Yoda

**walking
stick**

Meet Jar Jar Binks.
He is very clumsy.

ears

Jar Jar Binks

Meet Luke Skywalker.
He is a good pilot.

cape

Luke

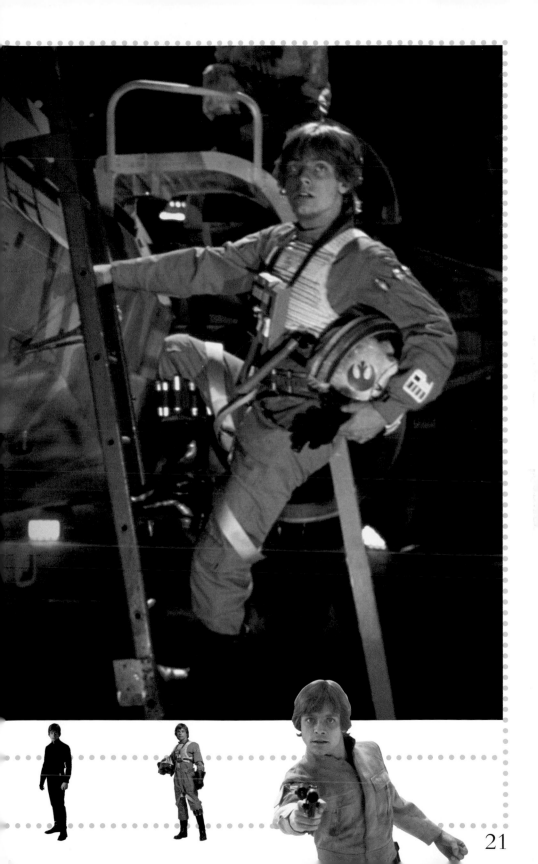

Meet Leia Organa.
She is a Princess.

uniform

Leia

blaster

Han

Meet Han Solo.
He is a pilot.
He flies a fast ship.

Meet Chewbacca.
He is a brave co-pilot.

fur

Chewbacca

Darth Vader

Meet Darth Vader.
He is a powerful villain.

helmet

Now you have met everyone.

Who is your favorite?

Glossary

Droid
another word for a robot

Jedi
a person who can use the Force

Lightsaber
a special sword with a blade made of light

Senator
a member of the galactic government

Villain
a bad person